Renew by phone or online

0845 0020 777

www.brist

Brist

D0343733

PLEASE RETURN B

A Note to Parents and Caregivers:

Read-it! Readers are for children who are just starting on the amazing road to reading. These beautiful books support both the acquisition of reading skills and the love of books.

The RED LEVEL presents familiar topics using common words and repeating sentence patterns.
The BLUE LEVEL presents new ideas using a larger vocabulary and varied sentence structure.
The YELLOW LEVEL presents more challenging ideas, a broad vocabulary, and wide variety in sentence structure.

When sharing a book with your child, read in short stretches, pausing often to talk about the pictures. Have your child turn the pages and point to the pictures and familiar words. And be sure to reread favorite stories or parts of stories.

There is no right or wrong way to share books with children. Find time to read with your child, and pass on the legacy of literacy.

Adria F. Klein, Ph.D.
Professor Emeritus
California State University
San Bernardino, California

First American edition published in 2003 by
Picture Window Books
5115 Excelsior Boulevard
Suite 232
Minneapolis, MN 55416
1-877-845-8392
www.picturewindowbooks.com

First published in Great Britain by Franklin Watts, 96 Leonard Street, London, EC2A 4XD
Text © Jillian Powell 2001
Illustration © Jayne Coughlin 2001

Printed in the United States of America.

Library of Congress Cataloging-in-Publication
Powell, Jillian.
  The lazy scarecrow / written by Jillian Powell ; illustrated by Jayne Coughlin.—1st
American ed.
    p. cm.—(Read-it! readers)
  Summary: After allowing the birds to eat all the seeds in his field, a lazy scarecrow realizes
the consequences of his behavior when summer comes and the field is bare.
  ISBN 1-4048-0062-X
  [1. Scarecrows—Fiction. 2. Laziness—Fiction.] I. Coughlin, Jayne, ill. II. Title. III. Series.
  PZ7.P87755 Laz 2003
  [E]—dc21   2002074935

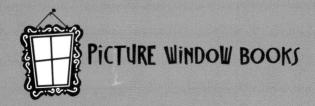

PICTURE WINDOW BOOKS

Read-it! Readers
Red Level

The Lazy Scarecrow

Written by Jillian Powell

Illustrated by Jayne Coughlin

Reading Advisors:
Adria F. Klein, Ph.D.
Professor Emeritus, California State University
San Bernardino, California

Ruth Thomas
Durham Public Schools
Durham, North Carolina

R. Ernice Bookout
Durham Public Schools
Durham, North Carolina

Picture Window Books
Minneapolis, Minnesota

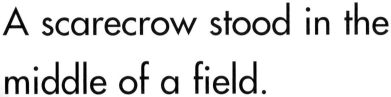

A scarecrow stood in the
middle of a field.

His job was to keep birds from eating the seeds.

But he was a very lazy scarecrow.

Soon, the birds came and began to eat the seeds.

"I don't care!" the scarecrow said.

They sat on his hat and on his arms.

Spring turned to summer,
and the field was bare.
All the seeds were gone!

The scarecrow was sad.
It was hot, and the wind
blew dust into his eyes.

He waved his arms around
and around.

The farmer came by in
his truck.

That scarecrow is working hard now, he thought.

So, the farmer moved the
scarecrow to a better field.

Green plants
danced around the
scarecrow's feet.

A bird came, and this time
the scarecrow waved his
arms to scare it away.

"Go away!" he shouted.
"Leave my plants alone!"

In the autumn, the plants were tall and strong.

It was the best harvest
the farmer had ever had.

He was so pleased, he gave the scarecrow a new hat for the winter.

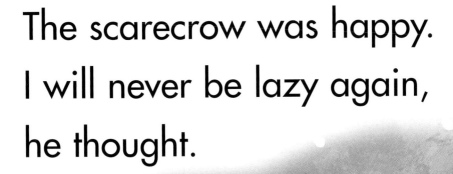

The scarecrow was happy.
I will never be lazy again,
he thought.

Red Level

The Best Snowman, by Margaret Nash 1-4048-0048-4
Bill's Baggy Pants, by Susan Gates 1-4048-0050-6
Cleo and Leo, by Anne Cassidy 1-4048-0049-2
Felix on the Move, by Maeve Friel 1-4048-0055-7
Jasper and Jess, by Anne Cassidy 1-4048-0061-1
The Lazy Scarecrow, by Jillian Powell 1-4048-0062-X
Little Joe's Big Race, by Andy Blackford 1-4048-0063-8
The Little Star, by Deborah Nash 1-4048-0065-4
The Naughty Puppy, by Jillian Powell 1-4048-0067-0
Selfish Sophie, by Damian Kelleher 1-4048-0069-7

Blue Level

The Bossy Rooster, by Margaret Nash 1-4048-0051-4
Jack's Party, by Ann Bryant 1-4048-0060-3
Little Red Riding Hood, by Maggie Moore 1-4048-0064-6
Recycled!, by Jillian Powell 1-4048-0068-9
The Sassy Monkey, by Anne Cassidy 1-4048-0058-1
The Three Little Pigs, by Maggie Moore 1-4048-0071-9

Yellow Level

Cinderella, by Barrie Wade 1-4048-0052-2
The Crying Princess, by Anne Cassidy 1-4048-0053-0
Eight Enormous Elephants, by Penny Dolan 1-4048-0054-9
Freddie's Fears, by Hilary Robinson 1-4048-0056-5
Goldilocks and the Three Bears, by Barrie Wade 1-4048-0057-3
Mary and the Fairy, by Penny Dolan 1-4048-0066-2
Jack and the Beanstalk, by Maggie Moore 1-4048-0059-X
The Three Billy Goats Gruff, by Barrie Wade 1-4048-0070-0